GOLLO
AND THE
LION

For Klara
—L.C.

Text and illustrations © 1994 by Albin Michel Jeunesse, France.
All rights reserved.
Printed in Italy.
© 1994 by Albin Michel Jeunesse, 22, rue Huyghens, 75014 Paris, France.
Original French title: *Gollo et le lion.*
First published in the United States of America in 1995 by Hyperion Books for Children,
114 Fifth Avenue, New York, New York 10011.

FIRST EDITION
1 3 5 7 9 10 8 6 4 2

Library of Congress Cataloging-in-Publication Data

Oyono, Éric.
Gollo and the lion/ Éric Oyono; illustrated by
Laurent Corvaisier — 1st ed.
p. cm.
Summary: In this folktale from Cameroon, Gollo goes to an old
soothsayer for help when Polgozom the lion devours his sister.
ISBN 0-7868-0041-0 (trade) — ISBN 0-7868-2034-9 (lib. bdg.)
(1. Folklore — Cameroon.   2. Brothers and sisters — Folklore.)
I. Corvaisier, Laurent, ill.   II. Gollo et le lion. English.
III. Title.
PZ8.1.O96Go 1994
398.21 — dc20
(E)
94-7276 CIP AC

The artwork for each picture is prepared using acrylic paint.
This book is set in 14-point Barcelona Bold.

ÉRIC OYONO

GOLLO
AND THE
LION

ILLUSTRATED BY
LAURENT CORVAISIER

HYPERION BOOKS FOR CHILDREN
NEW YORK

Once upon a time there lived a brother and sister. They made their home in a large forest near the edge of a windswept plain, called the savanna. Kaye tended their garden of millet and peanuts while her brother, Gollo, hunted and fished. Not a day went by when they weren't able to eat their fill.

Gollo left the hut early in the morning to go hunting and did not return until nightfall—and sometimes even later. Before he left he reminded Kaye to close the door tightly after dark so that no wild animals could get in.

Each evening Kaye listened for her brother's return. Before she would open the door she waited to hear him sing their special song:

Kaye, Kaye, O my sweet sister,
Open the door that I may come in.

When she recognized her brother's voice, Kaye would rush to welcome him, her bracelets jingling.

After supper Gollo would tell Kaye of that day's adventures. Stories of zebras, lions, and wildebeests filled Kaye's dreams all through the night. And so their life carried on happily from day to day.

A fierce and terrifying lion named Polgozom came to hear of Gollo and Kaye. He was a beast known to all the animals of the savanna for his ruthless greed and insatiable appetite. Polgozom began to hunger for the brother and sister and one day hid behind a tree just outside their hut. When night had fallen and the moon was high, the lion watched Gollo sing his special song to Kaye and heard the jingling of her bracelets as she rushed to the door. The following night he watched as they repeated their ritual.

On the third evening, before Gollo had returned, the lion emerged from his hiding place. As silently as possible, the big cat crept up to the door of the house and sang:

Kaye, Kaye, O my sweet sister,
Open the door that I may come in.

But his rough, raspy lion voice didn't fool Kaye.
She laughed and called:

That is not my brother's voice.
Go on your way, whoever you are!

Frustrated, Polgozom slunk away and climbed up a tree to think.
He thought and he thought, and just as dawn was breaking, he
came upon an idea.

Polgozom went to the edge of the river to look for Mother Crane. "Mother Crane," he said, "you must stroke the back of my throat with your long beak so that my voice will be smooth and gentle." Afraid to disobey the ferocious beast, the crane did as he asked. When Mother Crane had finished, Polgozom had a voice as sweet as honey.

Before the lion left, the wise crane warned, "Polgozom, your greedy appetite is legendary. Heed my advice and don't stop along the way to feed. Your new voice can be easily lost." The lion nodded his head impatiently and set out on his journey.

Very soon, however, he began to feel hungry and couldn't resist the urge to stop and eat a few bitter berries. When he arrived at Kaye and Gollo's house he sang:

Kaye, Kaye, O my sweet sister,
Open the door that I may come in.

But the berries had made his voice every bit as rough and raspy as before. Kaye laughed even louder at him this time as she replied:

That is not my brother's voice.
Go on your way, whoever you are!

Polgozom returned to Mother Crane to have his voice made gentle once again. "Perhaps there is something to your advice," the lion admitted. "My journey is long, and there are many temptations on the way. Command your son to ride on my back. Whenever I feel the urge to eat, he must peck me as a reminder to keep to my plan." Trembling, Mother Crane told her son to do as the beast demanded.

After enduring a number
of pecks from the little crane,
the lion finally arrived at Kaye's hut.
His stomach was empty, but his voice was
as clear and sweet as Gollo's. As he readied
himself to pounce, he sang out to Kaye:

> *Kaye, Kaye, O my sweet sister,*
> *Open the door that I may come in.*

As Kaye rushed to the door with bracelets jingling, the huge lion
sprang out of the darkness. Kaye had barely opened the door when
Polgozom flew through it and devoured her in one huge gulp. His
belly full, the beast lay down on the bed and soon drifted off to
sleep.

That evening Gollo returned from hunting. When he saw the
open door he became alarmed. Rushing in, he cried out in horror as
he caught sight of the lion, still asleep on the bed.

Polgozom awoke and, knowing Gollo's reputation as a fierce and skillful hunter, leaped out the window. As the lion fled, Gollo swung a huge knife over his head and shouted, "By Laouna, if that rotten beast has eaten my sister, let my knife cut off his cursed tail." Gollo hurtled his knife into the air, and the lion's tail was cut off.

Gollo cried for his sister all that night. When the sun rose over the savanna, he hurried to see the local soothsayer. The soothsayer was an ancient and wrinkled old man, known throughout the savanna for his wisdom as well as his magic. "As I see it," said the soothsayer, "your problem is twofold. You must determine which lion has swallowed Kaye. Next, you must force the beast to return her to you. Give me a little time to think about this problem; a lion can be a clever opponent."

The soothsayer thought hard for four days and four nights. On the morning of the fifth day, he woke Gollo and told him, "Take this gourd. You must cross the savanna and from every river, pool, and stream take one drop of water. When you are finished, dig a well at least a hundred times as deep as your height. Throw the gourd down into it. All the rivers and every pool and stream will instantly dry up. Next, climb up on the roof of your hut and call all the animals together with the promise that only you can bring back the water. In this way, you will have the force of all the thirsty beasts behind you when you confront the lion."

After thanking the soothsayer, Gollo set out on his task. He traveled thoughout the savanna collecting a drop of water from every river, pool, and stream.

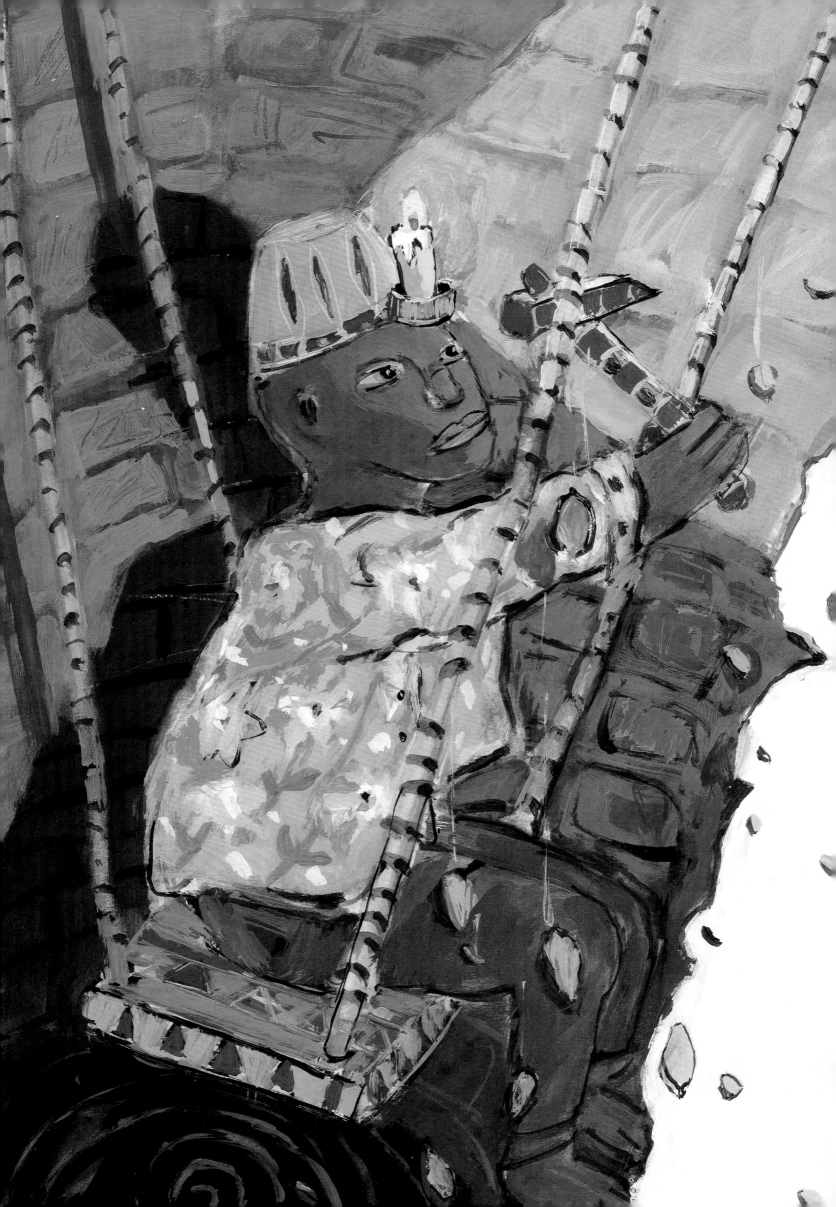

When he was done, Gollo returned home and dug the well. At nightfall he threw in the brimming gourd. Suddenly all the rivers ceased flowing, the pools turned to mud, and the streams became as dry as dust.

Just before dawn Gollo climbed onto the roof of his hut and shouted, "All you animals out there! The water has dried up, and I know you are thirsty. Come and show yourselves to me and I, Gollo, will tell you how to end this drought!" As daylight broke he saw before him every sort of animal in creation.

There were shorthaired, shaggy, and longhaired grass eaters; scaly, cold-blooded reptiles; panting beasts of prey; creatures that crawl in the dirt; and those that soar in the air.

Gollo knew that he had to be very clever to enlist the animals' help in returning Kaye. "Please listen to me!" he said. "I mean you no harm! On the contrary, I too want to bring back the water. But one of you has eaten my sister, and that is why I have caused this drought. When the animal whose tail I cut off returns her to me, only then will I make the water flow once more.

"All you birds," he commanded, "turn and present your tails to me!" In keeping with his plan, Gollo proclaimed that Kaye's killer was not among them and called the next group to come forward.

"Now, all you grass eaters and reptiles. Let me see your tails." After pretending to examine their tails, Gollo dismissed the group.

"Now, beasts of prey, come forward, turn your tails to me. Aha! Now I can see the beast who has eaten my sister and caused this drought!" And Gollo pointed his finger at the huge and mighty Polgozom, who had tried to trick him by making a tail out of straw.

The animals all circled menacingly around Polgozom, threatening him and demanding that he immediately return Kaye to Gollo before they all died of thirst. Shaken by this show of force, the frightened lion called out in a trembling voice:

O Kaye, sister of Gollo,
Return yourself from my belly!

With that, he threw back his head and gave a huge choking cough. But instead of Kaye, up from the lion's great belly came a big clay cooking pot.

"My sister is not a cooking pot," Gollo shouted. "Return her to me!"

Once again the lion threw back his head, repeated his words, and—*cough!*—an ancient tortoise appeared, his head still tucked inside his shell. Gollo's anger increased as he demanded Kaye's return. The trembling lion lowered his head and repeated his words a third time:

O Kaye, sister of Gollo,
Return yourself from my belly!

A tremendous shudder shook his entire body, and—*cough!*—there stood the beautiful Kaye, her bracelets jingling in the soft morning breeze. Gollo rushed to her, and the happy brother and sister hugged each other tight. Relieved and shaken, Polgozom slunk away into the dark forest.

As he had promised, Gollo told the animals how to
end the drought. "I have dug a well. The most agile
among you must go to the very bottom of it and bring up
a gourd that I have hidden there. Only then will the
water return."

The parrot, always a big talker, was the first to volun-
teer. But before he got very far he became frightened of
the cold, dark tunnel and hurried back into the sunlight.
The animals teased him for bragging and chose the
pigeon to try next. But even the pigeon, talented though
she was at traveling great distances, was not able to
reach the well's floor and was forced to turn back.

Growing agitated, the animals selected the strong and
graceful sparrow hawk to try to retrieve the precious
water gourd. The sparrow hawk first flew straight up
into the sky directly above the deep well. Then, folding
his wings and pointing his beak toward the ground, he
plunged through the air and into the well. Down, down
he went until at last he reached the bottom where lay
the gourd. Snatching it from the floor, he zoomed back
up through the dark tunnel and into the sky with the
gourd held firmly in his strong claws.

When he had soared so high that the animals on
the ground below became mere blurs of color and
shape, the hawk opened his claws and released the
gourd. When it hit the ground it broke into a thou-
sand pieces—and the pools swelled, the streams
became full, and the rivers rose up and flowed with
life once again. And safe in their forest hut on the
edge of the windswept savanna, Gollo and Kaye
smiled as they listened to the noisy, joyous celebra-
tion of the animals, welcoming the water's return.

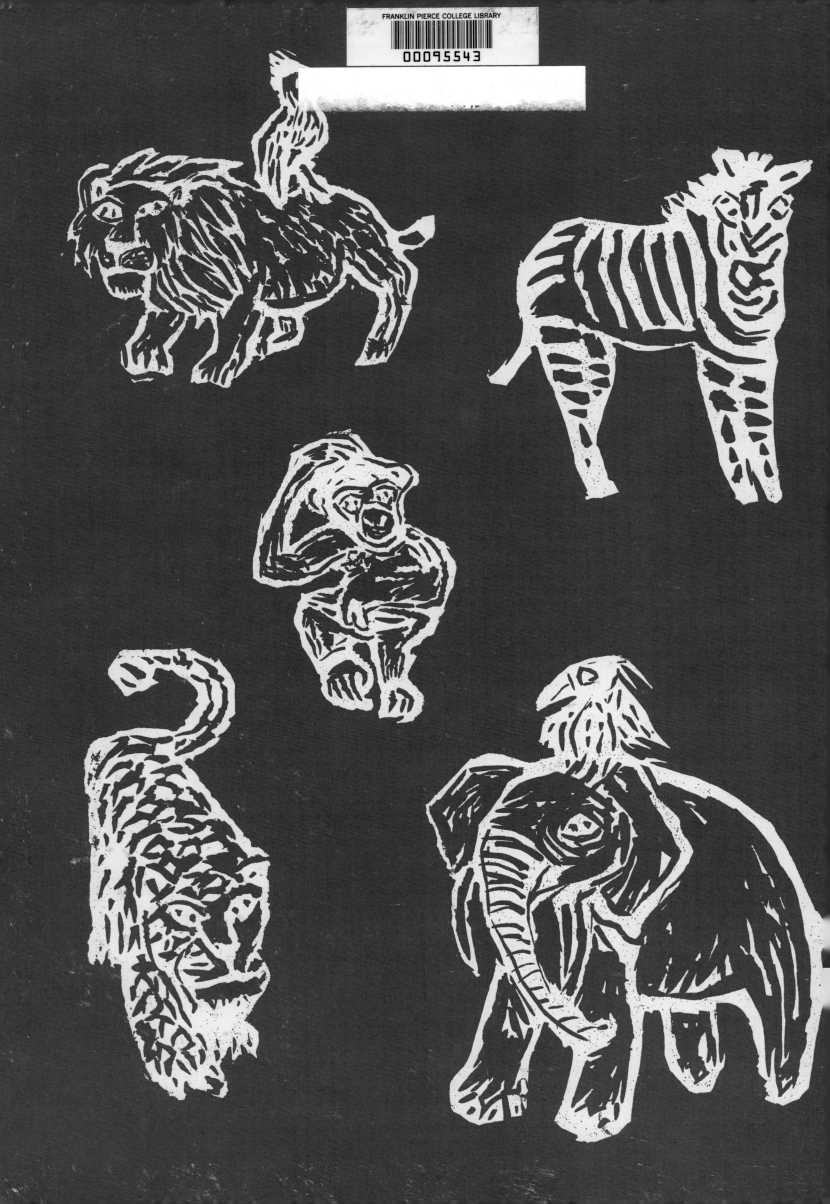